SHEEP, SHEEP, SHEEP,
Help Me Fall Asleep

written and with photographs by ARLENE ALDA

A Doubleday Book for Young Readers

Dundee Township Library
555 Barrington Avenue
Dundee, Illinois 60118-1498

A Doubleday Book for Young Readers
Published by Delacorte Press
Bantam Doubleday Dell Publishing Group, Inc.
666 Fifth Avenue
New York, New York 10103

Library of Congress Cataloging in Publication Data
Alda, Arlene. [date of birth]
Sheep, sheep, sheep, help me fall asleep / written and with
photographs by Arlene Alda.
p.   cm.
"A Doubleday book for young readers."
Summary: A child tries to fall asleep by counting sheep and sees a
variety of interesting animals before the wooly visitors show up.
ISBN 0-385-30791-8
[1. Bedtime—Fiction.   2. Sleep—Fiction.   3. Animals—Fiction.
4. Sheep—Fiction.   5. Stories in rhyme.]   I. Title.
PZ8.3.A35Sh   1992
[E]—dc20   91-43006   CIP   AC

Designed by Jane Byers Bierhorst
Text set in 17 point ITC Berkeley Old Style Medium
Manufactured in the United States of America
November 1992
10 9 8 7 6 5 4
WOR

To giggles and rhymes
And family times

With special thanks to
Tabatha, Briony, Joe Henson,
John Croft, and Paul Donohue of
the Windsor Safari Park,
England.

I saw a very itchy cow

I couldn't fall asleep one night.
My mommy said, "That's quite all right.
Just close your eyes and look for sheep.
Then count them and you'll fall asleep."
I closed my eyes the way she said.
I didn't see the sheep; instead...

A cat too busy to meow

A hairy gorilla who tickled her toes

And piglets in mud, which they liked, I suppose.

I saw those animals, none of them sheep—
Well, that seemed better than falling asleep.
I stretched and whispered, "Boy, this is fun.
Before I see sheep, the night will be done."
Then a fat hippo smiled. (I wondered what for.)

And a goat played peek-a-boo out her front door.

Some geese went out walking, all in a line.

A horse started talking. (His voice was like mine!)

I got awfully tired while looking for sheep,
But somehow or other, I still couldn't sleep.
I wiggled, I squirmed, I turned and I tossed.
Where were the sheep? Could they have been lost?

At last I saw one. It had wooly hair.

Then there were two of them. That made a pair.

I counted to three. I looked for some more.

My eyelids were heavy when there were four.

Five sheep. Now six.

Then seven

and eight.

Nine came along. I think it was late.

I yawned a big yawn and counted to ten.
There were too many sheep to start counting again.

I finally slept like a lamb—yes, that's true.

But oh how I wished for a big kangaroo!